D0591230

This book belongs to:

All Ladybird books are available at most bookshops,
supermarkets and newsagents, or can be ordered direct from:

Ladybird Postal Sales
PO Box 133 Paignton TQ3 2YP England
Telephone: (+44) 01803 554761
Fax: (+44) 01803 663394

A catalogue record for this book is available
from the British Library

Published by Ladybird Books Ltd
A subsidiary of the Penguin Group
A Pearson Company

Text © Joan Stimson MCMXCVIII
Illustrations © Cliff Wright MCMXCVIII

LADYBIRD and the device of a Ladybird are trademarks of
Ladybird Books Ltd Loughborough Leicestershire UK

Are We Nearly There?

by Joan Stimson
illustrated by Cliff Wright

Ladybird

Today was the day for Daisy and Dad's journey.

Daisy had been staying with her grandparents.
But now Dad had come to collect her, and to
take her somewhere even more special!

Daisy couldn't wait to set off. So, as soon as they had said their goodbyes, she began to run –

along the twisty track ...

At first Daisy ran as fast as she could. But, little by little, she began to tire.

"Are we nearly there?" asked Daisy. "It's Rabbit," she explained. "He's too *tired* to go any further."

Dad shook his head. But he tucked Rabbit
on top of their rucksack. And Daisy padded off –

along the twisty track ...

Daisy and Dad padded side by side.

But suddenly something rumbled.

"Are we nearly there?" shouted Daisy above the noise. "It's my tummy," she explained. "It's too *empty* to go any further!"

Dad shook his head. But he rummaged in their rucksack and found the food.

Daisy ate all her own picnic and most of Dad's. For a while she was too *full* to go any further. So Daisy had a little snooze. And before long she felt light enough to dance –

along the twisty track …

But Daisy wasn't looking where she was dancing. She didn't see the bed of nettles!

"OW, WOW, WOUCH! Are we nearly there?" wailed Daisy. "It's my paws," she explained. "They're too *hot and stingy* to go any further!"

Dad shook his head. But he blew and he blew until Daisy's paws were cool again and she could bounce –

along the twisty track …

Dad was just getting into *his* bounce when there was a crackle of lightning.

Next there was a crash of thunder.
And then as soon as the thunder and lightning
had stopped it began to pour with rain.

Daisy didn't like getting wet.

"Are we n-n-nearly th-th-th-there?"
she shivered. "It's my fur," explained Daisy.
"It's too *soggy* to go any further!"

Dad shook his head. But he rummaged in their rucksack and brought out a towel.

"Rub-a-dub-dub. Rub-a-dub-dub," went Dad, until his arms ached and Daisy was warm and dry.

"Ooooh, look!" cried Daisy. "It's a rainbow!"
And she skipped towards it –

along the twisty track ...

The sun grew warm, then hot

"Phew! Are we nearly there?" panted Daisy. "It's *meee*," she explained. "I'm too *floppy* to go any further."

Dad flopped down, too. "So am I!" he said.

"Oh, no!" cried Daisy. "Now we'll *never* get there!"

But Dad was already rummaging... right to the bottom of their rucksack.

At last he found what he wanted...

"It's a bottle of Grandma's Famous Fizz,"
he beamed. "She told me to keep it for
emergencies."

Dad held the bottle in a stream to cool it.

"Mmmm!" said Daisy and Dad. And they
drank exactly half each.

As soon as they'd finished their fizz, Dad swung Daisy onto his shoulders. Then he carried her –

round the final twist in the track...

And suddenly Daisy could see for herself.
"Look, Dad, look," she cried, "WE'RE NEARLY
THERE! WE'RE NEARLY THERE!"

Dad set Daisy gently on the ground.

"Come *on!*" she told him.

And together they ran the rest of the way –

to the end of the twisty track …

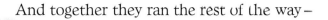

HOME!